The Secret No-Girls Club

Rachel Elizabeth Cole

Illustrated by Kathrina Iris

Tangled Oak Press, 2015

ISBN: 9780994821614

Cover by Littera Designs

First Edition

For my boys

Table of Contents

1
Club Rules

Caleb and Logan wanted to start a club.

They met in Logan's tree house after school.

They pulled up the ladder and closed the trap door.

They sat on crates around the old play table and got down to business.

"It has to be a no-girls club," Caleb said.

"Yeah, a secret no-girls club,"
Logan agreed.

First they needed to make the
rules. Caleb pulled out a piece of
lined paper and a pencil from his
backpack.

The Rules

Rule #1: No Girls a loud.

Rule #2: You have to keep the Secrit No Girls Club a secrit.

Rule #3: Sombody has to stand gard so no Girls try to get in.

Rule #4: You have to use the Secrit Handshack and the Secrit Passwerd to get in.

Rule #5: Nobody goes to the bath room with out asking.

Rule #6: Be nise to everybody but not Girls.

Next they created a secret password: "Girls are gross!"

Then they created a secret handshake: three armpit farts in a row, then a burp, then a high five.

They practiced it until they were laughing so hard they started hiccupping.

Then they wrote a pledge. They practiced it until they started mixing it up and couldn't say it right anymore.

"I do slalomly promise to . . . Oh, I can't remember now!" Caleb said.

"Always and forever . . ." Logan prompted him.

"Oh right. To always and forever keep The Secret No-Girls Club a secret and to never let a girl get in."

"Never *ever* let a girl get in." Logan corrected.

"Never ever!" Caleb said.

Finally, they had to decide who was president.

"I'll be president," Caleb said.

"You can't choose to be president!" Logan said. "You have to be elected."

"Says who?"

"My dad."

Logan's dad was a lawyer so he knew all about these things.

"Okay, then how do you get elected?" Caleb asked.

"You have an election!" Logan said.

2
The Election

The boys found an old shoebox and cut a slot in the top.

They cut up some paper and made ballots with a check box beside each of their names.

Then they secretly filled out the ballots and put them in the box.

"Make sure you don't show who you're voting for," Logan said.

Then Caleb took the lid off the box and drew out the ballots.

One vote for Caleb. One vote for
Logan.

"That didn't work," Caleb said.

"Okay," Logan said. "We'll do it again. Only we can't vote for ourselves."

"Good idea." Caleb nodded.

They made more ballots.

This time, Logan drew them out of the box.

One vote for Caleb. One vote for Logan.

"This isn't working!" Caleb cried. "Can't I just be president?"

"No way!" Logan shook his head. He thought for a moment. "We need a neutral party."

"A what?"

"Somebody whose name isn't on the ballots."

The boys went to the tree house window.

Logan's twin sister, Isabella, was playing with her stuffed animals in the backyard below.

She glanced up at the tree house.

They ducked down quick before she saw them.

"No way!" Caleb said. "She's a girl!"

"Wait! I know!" Logan said. "Your little brother."

"But Jonah can't even read yet," Caleb said.

"That's okay, he can just tick one of the boxes," Logan said. "Go get him."

Caleb opened the trap door and lowered the ladder. Then he ran next door to get Jonah.

3
A Neutral Party

"A secret no-girls club?" Jonah tossed aside his toy cars. "Cool!"

So they made Jonah a Junior Member of The Secret No-Girls Club.

They read him the rules.

They made him practice the secret handshake and password.

They made him say the pledge.

They explained to Jonah how voting worked. And then they each filled out new ballots and put them into the box.

This time, Caleb drew the ballots.

One vote for Caleb. One vote for Logan. One vote for . . . Caleb and Logan?

"Jonah!" Caleb cried. "You're not supposed to vote for both of us!"

"You said tick the boxes!" Jonah said. "I ticked the boxes!"

"This isn't working." Logan paced the floor of the tree house. "We need another plan."

Just then, the trap door swung open.

Isabella's blonde head popped up through the hole in the floor. "What are you guys doing?"

"Nothing!" Caleb and Logan cried.

"Go away! It's a secret club!" Jonah said.

"Jonah!" Caleb and Logan cried.

"A secret club? Can I join?" Isabella said.

"No way!" Logan said. "It's The Secret No-Girls Club! No girls allowed!"

"But I'm not a girl. I'm your sister," Isabella said, with a hurt look.

She started to close the trap door and climb back down the ladder.

"Wait!" Caleb said. "If we let you join the club, will you vote for who gets to be president?"

Isabella tapped her chin as she thought it over.

"Okay," she said.

So they made Isabella a Member of The Secret No-Girls Club.

They read her the rules.

They made her practice the secret handshake and password.

They made her say the pledge.

"Okay, let's vote," Caleb said.

This time, Logan drew the ballots.

One vote for Caleb. One vote for Logan. Two votes for . . . Isabella?

"But . . . but . . . but . . ." Caleb and Logan said.

But the ballots didn't lie.

Isabella had been elected the very first president of The Secret No-Girls Club.

"We need a new club." Logan sighed. "A Super-Secret No-Girls Club."

"I'll be president," Caleb said.

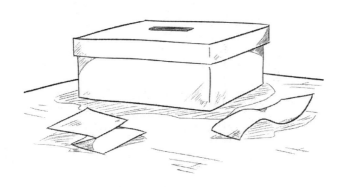

Also by the Author

The Kids in the Tree House Series

The Backyard Bug Hunters (Book 2)

The Rabbit Ate My . . . Series

The Rabbit Ate My Homework (Book 1)

The Rabbit Ate My Flip-Flops (Book 2)

About the Author

Rachel Elizabeth Cole writes a mix of genres, from heartfelt to humorous, but her favourite will always be children's fiction. Rachel's favourite season is autumn, she prefers tea to coffee, and wishes every morning began at ten a.m. Even though she hates the rain, Rachel lives just outside Vancouver, British Columbia, with her husband, their two sons, and two very spoiled house rabbits.

Acknowledgements

Thanks always to my family and friends and loved ones for your continued support and encouragement. Thanks also to those who contributed to making this book a reality, including my talented illustrator, Kathrina Iris. And thanks to everyone at Backspace, the SCWBI Blueboards, the KBoards, CritClub, and the various other private groups I've been a part of over the years for the guidance, help, and a good kick in the behind when I need it.

Made in the USA
Lexington, KY
13 November 2016